These are Frank Hildebrandt's words written over many years starting around the early '70's. Words and thoughts about the passing days of what came to his mind. They aren't in any special order, just inside for seeing the many years he felt at any given moment of time. Words sometimes on scraps of paper or a cocktail napkin. Saved for sharing to anyone's reading.

Some are written from his yearly Christmas cards sent to people that he has known over the years.

These may be his last writings!

Thoughts Along The Way

Frank Hildebrandt

About the Author

For 46+ years, I've had a career in Law Enforcement. A dream I had since I was a little kid. Dreams sometimes do come true. Now that I am retired, I thought perhaps it was time to share these writings. So much time has passed. Most were written for someone special; shared, but most times not. Private thoughts that touched or were felt by me. Some did get shared, most not. Words were written down, hidden with some still sad. Most times, forgotten and filed away.

Never really forgotten.

Thoughts Along The Way

UNTITLED

May every door ahead,

open as you go.

And the ones you've

passed - stay ajar.

If for no other reason,

then to look back –

While always going on.

UNTITLED

Words that never

will be spoken.

Are sounds that

never will be heard.

Letters that never

will be written.

Are thoughts that

never will be read.

UNTITLED

There is a time for laughter,

    and there is a time for tears,

for each of us has happy days,

    and days when grief appears.

But we have our troubles,

    just as when we're glad and gay,

we should always remember,

    that this, too, will pass away.

THE "GG" TRAIN (QUEENS OF BROOKLYN)

The ride
 was longer than usual.

I felt it would last,

beyond the time

I had remaining.

To be late,

the excuse

couldn't be told.

Lights flash by.

It's late. No,

the sun hasn't risen.

I'm alone

this morning.

I felt it when I left.

My head still filled

there's nothing inside.

LOOK BACK

Sometimes,

    as we pass

        through this life

    a person catches

          a passing smile

            as we move by.

Thoughts are exchanged,

    then passed back.

As they entangle

    the closeness becomes

           apparent

        But, life

           with a pace that

    cannot stand still

      allows each person

many paths.

Roads to nowhere, yet

ever moving to somewhere.

And yes,

sometimes back to

the beginning...

the smile.

August 1985

HER EYES

W hen I look

    and see you

        looking,

your eyes show me

    something unique

        for the first time.

Perhaps, it's the

        way you're able

    to let me know

  the feelings enclosed.

Maybe it's not intended

    to show feeling

        to me,

    but

I hope to

grasp the glance,

even for that
                brief second.

Please look back.

I never looked

        away.

August 1985

THE ESCAPE

An affair

    is something

        I use

  for the journey.

The journey

    which I have

  taken before,

      and

    returned alone.

Unsure,

    I need the thought

      you're coming.

Don't ask,

    I don't know the course.

What I purpose

is uncertainty

that

I'll ever escape.

Let's draw a map.

February 1987

THE WEEKEND

Did I say

thank you?

It seems

we steal,

for the weekends

from a week

of lost treasures.

We take each

others dreams

into a single

move.

Moving forward

in the discovery

of the end — and

beginning of the

    search

        through

  another week,

        for a glimpse

  of the thought

        a weekend,

    will come

        again....

And again.

UNTITLED

I'm in love

      with a dream.

Not so much

         with you,

    as the thought

        of you.

I know it's not love

but, I grasp for

        the dreams

    of a man in love.

Not with love.

I'll always dream,

    of you.

UNTITLED

A year passes

    with a bunk

        of an eye.

Only by

    keeping them

        open,

  can I slow time.

I just haven't learned,

    to dream with

        open eyes.

UNTITLED

As I pass AMCH

  her memory is

      felt.

I know she

      wasn't always mine

  but, there was

      a time I thought

          she was.

Deep inside me her

  love is there.

Now as I walk

              by,

  thinking only of

      the many times

I was here.

In my memories,

she will

always be mine.

I now share her,

with no one.

UNTITLED

W hen,

    I try to talk

        with my feelings,

you never understand.

Do I expect

        too much

   from a relationship

         with you?

I'm trying

        to be more open,

   than you're

         able to accept.

Maybe,

   maybe not.

I took you

        as a precious stone.

MY BIRTHDAY

Next year

I'll spend it different.

Only each year

has become

a repeat,

of the ones past.

Next year,

I'll spend it different.

March 1989

YOU MY FRIEND

Some people

  come into

    our lives

and leave,

    leaving us with

      many memories.

You my friend,

      have

    left me

      much to remember.

Memories,

    which tomorrow

      we can

remember…..

      You and I.

YESTERDAY GONE BY

Yesterday's belong

    to one's past.

You can go back,

    but you cannot

    live ---

        time gone by.

 Use your dreams

    to relive your memories

 of the days

    that have gone

        by.

Life is meant

    to be lived for today

 which is to become,

        tomorrow.

GIRAFFES

Giraffes are able

    to reach much

higher than I.

    Unlike the

  giraffes, I didn't understand

the extent of my reach.

I respect that, but

  don't understand

     why …..

THE AIRPORT

Moving through

the airport

I feel alone.

People rush to

lines, few smile

only to wait.

Planes come

and go.

New people rush

by. All

going somewhere. Some

going nowhere.

What seems

to be the same?

As we fly

from this place

to that.

I had a plan

or thought.

We expect and

surely know

no such plan

will always follow through.

I had a plan,

what happened?

THE PASSING OF A DAISY

Now it's winter.

Cold, silent, lonely -----

    as I look out

        into the fields,

    snow covers the ground.

As sure as spring rains

        she will be back.

Reaching higher,

    greener than blades

        of grass.

Grasping the yellow

        in the golden sun ----

she will still retain,

        the white of

winter's edge.

Calling to her

      now,

           through

the howling winter

       winds.

She will not respond

     to my voice.

She follows

     not me,

   she is too gentle

to fight the wind.

        But,

Spring is near.

The rain will replace

     the snow,

   the wind will pass.

   Passing on winter

to spring,

      she will come.

The sun will lift

      her into the air.

Drops of rain warmed

    by the sun, moves

    her into life.

Each day a little closer

    yet, nearer to

      when she will go.

The rains have stopped

    and the suns light,

    lets me see her.

Summer is the time

she enjoys most.

Watching her beauty now

is hard to hold.

If I grasp her gentle

frame, she will die.

But, leaving her there

winter will again take

her away.

Summer must give way

to Fall.

Should I let her fade

into the winter wind,

or

take hold

now, and hope?

Maybe

if I gave her love

she would not die.

The winter will take

her back.

I'll reach out

again

for her.

If the winter takes her

before I reach the fields,

she will be gone.

Maybe she will come again

and again

But, somehow I think -----

this **Daisy**, may not.

The fields are

within sight.

Feeling chilled,

    my heart now subtle

   by the coming wind

      that winter always

              brings.

Just this once,

     couldn't winter

   be late….

UNTITLED

Now,

for the second time

I find myself alone.

Alone in a time

when a man needs

a warm hand, a

tender touch, understanding,

but most of all

love.

Man can not

exist without it,

nor should he try.

I look within every woman,

but never find the

complete person I want.

Could it be I ----- who

must change.

Some have said yes,

many have said no.

I think not.

I want what is felt.

It's the feeling that

is not right..

I could give, if----

only you were right.

I will keep looking,

but how long will it take?

Maybe that question is

 incorrect or words wrong.

I know time as a measurement

does not apply----I have

to put it another

way.

Which way?

UNTITLED

For each day we live

there will have been

     a yesterday.

Remember each day vividly

   forgetting

     not the smallest detail.

Don't allow the

   tomorrow's ahead----

To be empty of dreams

     of the days gone by.

THE LETTER THAT NEVER CAME

I waited for your letter.

No, it hasn't come

yet ---- maybe tomorrow.

She will surely send

a Christmas card ---- she's

good that way you know.

DISCARDED TREASURES

W alking along the beach

   I see how life

         moves along

   the water's edge.

Washing in upon

      the shore

   then out ---- leaving

               treasures to be found,

discarded by the sea.

Some are again reclaimed

                and lost,

      most again

         discarded by the sea.

Treasures for those of us

        who seek them

to be saved in another

        corner of our world.

Only later

        to be discarded

    and just maybe .....

        again reclaimed.

UNTITLED

Sadness never seems

    to totally end

  these last few years.

I must put together

      my life

  to reach a

    point of living.

The thought of

  giving up, is

    considered more often.

What sanity I still possess

  keeps me moving.

If that little bit

was to be drained

now ----

The struggle would

be over.

UNTITLED

As I am

    greeted by the

        sun

the desire for

        living becomes

    more evident.

If only the

        sun could shine,

    everyday.

WINDY NIGHT

As I sit,

    passing time

        with the wind,

the night brings

    moments of loneliness.

The feeling felt,

    when you move from

        my eyes.

I look for you

  and know you're safe,

  but not within my

    reach.

You're like the wind.

Moving away, then back.

When you're near

   the warmth holds

        me within your arms.

 As you let go

   the wind returns --

let go as you must

   but, come back to me

        before the night

   gives way.

UNTITLED

I have chosen

    my profession....

You have trained

    me well....

We have given

    our best....

Now dear lord

    give me rest.

UNTILTED

Moments are

no longer moments.

They've come

together and

now---years

have passed.

Time builds

more distance,

then miles could

ever hope to do.

We can not move

back in time,

but miles can

be overcome.

Run this way----

and hope.

UNTITLED

My life

    seems to reach

        for more

            then I can find.

Why ----

    after all these

           years,

      haven't I been

    able to settle?

It's as if

    I am lost,

somewhere between

    yesterday and today.

Tomorrow will have

to bring the answer,

or the end.

UNTITLED

How do you say

to someone,

"I am losing you"?

Or perhaps

that's wrong, because

I have lost you.

Maybe not to him

or even the one

before that.

It's

more likely to be,

the one tomorrow.

And that,

not even I can stop

nor you.

But that lost,

if even recovered,

would never belong----

To me.

LAST NIGHT

Last night

wasn't easy,

and this morning

was even worse.

Tomorrow morning

hasn't come,

maybe it will stay away

just this once.

UNTITLED

You remember the dreams

I had that first

day we met?

They say

it's good to dream you know.

I'm not so sure,

sometimes they're just

Dreams.

UNTITLED

Loneliness

    of unbearable magnitude

        has entered my life.

Far greater then

    even I

        had anticipated,

  or

knew possible.

Now,

    unable to deal

        with it,

    I must act.

I find myself lost.

Never have I

seen life,

so empty.

January 1978

THE SUN …. IS SHE

The sun

    seems to give way

to allow me

       another day.

I think back

    wondering why,

the last moments

       moved by so rapidly?

Then it's over.

It's recaptured,

         loved

again

lost to the night.

Now,

with a mere blink

of my eyes

my memories

hold

the sun.

If only

for that once,

why couldn't….

No.

Like the sun

she

will always come

and will always go.

Tomorrow

   I know the sun

      will come again.

THE TORTOISE AND THE LADY

Life, comes and goes.

Each day passes

with time moving,

unable to slow

to my pace.

I have not known

the speed of others.

My motion slow,

as I wander with

the journey of time.

Somehow in the journey

the nearness of others,

a stranger to me.

Upon my shoulders

I struggle, with the

burden of my life.

It's not easy

traveling slowly and alone.

She must have needed

a place to rest,

and I, her touch.

Now she, no added

burden to my life.

Rides with me,

through the journey

 of time.

UNTITLED

Listen,

I'm here.

Don't leave me yet.

Where do I go?

How do I pay?

1977

SHE DOESN'T KNOW

W ho is he?

I can't make him go,

nor let him stay.

I can't put him down,

nor pick him up.

Yet,

why is he here?

I should know.

He knows.

Why not me?

Frank why?

UNTITLED

I plea for life

for death is close.

I can see it

yet, I can't look.

It's felt by me.

But, yet untouched.

It's here ---- next to me.

My breath short.

Darkness fills my eyes,

I no longer see.

My hand motionless

it's ended.

I'm dead.

UNTITLED

If man -----

Was to stop,

life is said to end.

UNTITLED

Listen to the sounds.

It's like you can feel

the chill, and

not merely the wind.

UNTITLED

I look back

at life

one could say,

to remember.

Life is made

of memories.

What was past

and what will pass.

Today somehow

leaves me to believe,

that my memories

lie within that past.

THE APARTMENT

Days have passed

since I was there.

I drove by today

only to remember yesterday,

or was it

the day before?

Time passes and we forget

somehow I remember.

Everyone sees the sign

"Apartment for Rent."

I was there, but

then so was she

at **255**.

UNTITLED

As sure as the sun

      comes up each

  morning,

another day will

  get a new

      beginning.

YOU AND I ARE DIFFERENT.

It's hard to believe..

I'm not sure why

I guess,   no.

Maybe I'm different.

I would think

if only people would look.

You must be different.

To be the same

you see nothing,

outside your vision.

I want to see

beyond the farthest mountain.

To use only one's eyes

you lack the difference,

between you and I.

UNTITLED

As I find myself

    sad and lonely,

I just think

    about the days

        gone by.

I possess

    the power

  to recall all

    my yesterdays.

Reliving them

    one by one

  in my mind.

The reason is

    we are alive.

  And there will always

be a tomorrow.

So today,

    will become a yesterday

        that can be remembered,

            or

just forgotten.

But never forget -----

There will always

    be memories,

    of the tomorrow's ahead.

UNTITLED

T oday, as yesterday

will never be reclaimed.

For once something

is gone

this perhaps, is

when we must find

something in its place.

Love too becomes

lost, but we somehow

someway replace that.

But, in the replacement

what was passed

is still there.

For-----

Love that is received

is never truly forgotten!

UNTITLED

I f,

I was to touch

you again.

I'm sure it would

be the same.

Remembering --- the parts

that were made

to be touched.

And the parts,

made only to be

held---

The handle bars ---------

UNTITLED

Sometimes,

there comes a time

when people need.

And, with each need

want someone. And

with this want,

which may come

at any time.

Seems to come

at the end,

Christmas is said

to come at the

end,

of December.

So this Christmas,

I need and want

you.

I'm people----

UNTITLED

A birthday---

Which comes once

in any given year.

Is never remembered

by many, other

than the person

forgotten.

More than not,

it is remembered.

But,

not at the right time.

So I send this card today

for the many

Happy Birthday's of

yesterday----

SEEDS

If we were

to collect -----

A few seeds everyday,

and save them

until it rains.

On that day,

we could start

from the beginning.

Each seed has

the power of life.

So life can start

when we begin.

UNTITLED

I find it hard

to remember.

Not of you,

which is something

that can't be

forgotten. But ------

Of the last time

we touched.

It seems to be

such a long time ago -----

THE LOSS OF A DAISY

I passed by the field

    and thought of you.

Never have I seen

      so many before.

Could I hold

    the beauty I could see?

As I made my way

    I wanted to grasp

  each and every one.

I tried as you see,

      but

  none are mine.

Take what I have

seen. They are yours.

I remember

  each time I pass,

but a single one.

  Or by just

  thinking of you.

UNTITLED

As I find myself

       sad and lonely,

I just think

  about the days

          gone by.

I possess

  the power

to recall all

      my yesterdays.

Reliving them

      one by one

  in my mind.

The reason is

      we are alive.

  And there will always

be a tomorrow.

So today,

　　will become a yesterday

　　　　that can be remembered

　　　　　　or

just forgotten.

But never forget---

There will always

　　　　be memories,

of the tomorrows ahead.

January 31, 2006

WHERE HAVE THE FLOWÉRS GONE?

The Flowérs

    have come

        and gone…

We had, but

  a short time

     to watch them grow.

I got to know,

    her smile

  for too short

      of time.

No one knows

    just how long

Flowérs will

grow.

Perhaps if we

let them go

wild

on their own,

they could survive.

No one knows

just how long

Flowérs will

grow.

I had thought

that,

that this Flowér

won't die.

She gave me

so much joy,

in the colors

of her

smile.

"… do you know

how much I love

you?..." seemed

to be

what echoed from

her smile.

How did the

sunshine

leave us so soon?

No one knows

just how long

Flowérs will

grow.

For my wife,

Marléne Michael who

was always my Flowérs

CONTENTS:

1985

IT'S COLD, AND CHRISTMAS

The snow has

started

and the night has come,

lying across the sky

as a cold blanket.

I feel chilled,

seeing the wind

blow the snow against

my window.

Looking out into the

winter's night

I think of so many

moments…

yet past,

and some that

I hope to come.

It's Christmas,

and the snow

is most welcome tonight.

People are locked inside

with friends,

loves and loves that might

have been,

but never will.

I dream upon

each snowflake

and watch them disappear

within the night sky,

only to be rebuilt

upon the ground.

I now drift,

    as with the snow.

  Drift as we may tonight

      upon the snow

in front of our eyes

      memories fade,

  blending amidst the snow

      then only to be set

        adrift,

      by the wind.

Behind my window

    the wind reminds me

      it's cold, and Christmas.

People are locked inside

    with friends,

  loves and loves that might

      have been,

but never will.

1985

GLIMPSE OF CHRISTMAS PAST

The ground is

    covered with

        snow.

    As I walk and

        remember

    years back,

Christmas was so

    much different

        back then.

Windows are dressed

    with lights blinking

        a warm welcome

    as I pass by.

Inside one catches

a glimpse of faces,

      smiles and friends.

As I stand

      staring,

   I feel warm

      as the wind blows

         against my face.

It's cold,

   and as the snow

      falls,

   I'm reminded I must

      move on.

Down the road

   home waits,

      and it's Christmas.

1986

THE NIGHT BEFORE

The sun

   moves down

making way for the

   evening stars.

The night is chilled,

     with

   the light snow

that falls upon my

        face.

The rush of people

    leaving the

      stores,

  pushing past

with the last

minute treasures.

As I walk,

the familiar bell

is ringing.

The little woman dressed

in red

requesting a bit of

sharing,

that comes with Christmas.

The snow is a little

heavier now,

as it builds under

each step.

A little closer to

home,

where one will find

the outstretched arms

of friends and loves

        we will share,

    this Christmas

        season with.

1986

CHRISTMAS REVEALED

As I sit,

   my eyes

      once again

   gaze into the

        fireplace.

I ponder,

      as I watch

   the fire flicker.

The familiar smells

      of Christmas

   fill the air.

Slowly drifting,

I imagine

    the thoughts

of Christmas morning.

Packages being opened,

    the anticipation of

        discovering dreams,

    the disappointment of

        forgotten hopes.

Thinking back,

    thoughts

        of so many years

            drift past.

As the fire crackles,

    I'm brought

        back.

Tomorrow is Christmas.

    And

so come the dreams

　　　　and hopes

　　we will discover,

this Christmas season.

1988

CHRISTMAS MAGIC

As I turned

another page,

drifting

the book

I held

felt heavy,

as I

was

made

warm by

the

fire.

My mind turned

from the printed pages,

to the thoughts

of Christmas.

Christmas for most,

had started.

Not much like

years ago,

when we thought

Santa Claus brought

the MAGIC,

the boxes under

the trees,

and the joy

in people's hearts.

I guess I fell

asleep

in this old soft chair.

But,

I seem to remember

the lights on the

tree were out.

And those gifts---

As I looked up

rubbing my eyes,

I saw her smiling.

"It's MAGIC," she said

with a smile

and a ho ho ho.

I knew then,

as long as

one believes,

Christmas is the MAGIC

within all of

us.

1990

FOR YET ANOTHER YEAR

The smell of

pine has faded

for yet another year.

The holidays have passed,

and we remember

the excitement which was

built into a

single morning.

Perhaps it's good Christmas

comes but once a year.

Leaving us with

undisappointed dreams

lasting throughout the year.

Oh yes, just as we

    move through

the months until the

    magic comes back,

we shall not forget.

The reminders are found,

    rediscovered, lost

  within the many corners

of our lives.

The glimmer is unmistaken.

That piece of tinsel

    curled in that corner,

      overlooked, forgotten.

Tucked away with those

    undisappointed dreams.

And,

   left in place

      for yet another year.

1991

SEARCHING AT CHRISTMAS

W here was it that

we went

in search of a tree?

I remember that walk

so long ago.

The December air hinted

that Christmas was near.

The cold wasn't felt then,

only the thoughts

of Christmas.

We made our way

and somehow knew,

which one to cut.

Does it always happen

that way?

That tree was long ago

discarded,

that Christmas

has passed years of others,

and now,

to another…

We no longer walk

through those woods

in search of a tree.

We found it that year.

I guess I did discover

many things then.

Just what they were

    are now left to memories.

I wonder if people

    still do that,

    search for a tree?

1994

A GIFT FOR CHRISTMAS

In and out

of the stores,

we search

to discover the joy,

that one special offering

to share with another

and another.

What is it,

that makes us search endlessly

until we find it?

Do we ever find

that special gift

of sharing?

Maybe it's really out

        in the open.

Perhaps inside our thoughts

           or

    wrapped within

        our hearts.

Gifts at Christmas

    are not always within paper.

      To be unwrapped with hands

        paper discarded.

    Most times,

they're stored within us.

    Shared,

  given away

    and maybe taken back.

The real gifts

    at Christmas

are always within us.

Passed with a mere glance,

   a spoken word,

      a smile.

It's not for sale,

   held or

      unwrapped.

It's felt between us.

1994

CHRISTMAS BACK THEN

It's not yet morning,

    it's dark,

  the light hasn't crept in

      between the curtain

        openings.

The windows always seemed

    to have had frost on them.

      I remember our windows

       had shades.

    Did they have window blinds

      back then?

My brother slept

    below me

on the lower bunk.

My sister

in the other room,

no others.

They came later,

my little brother

and sister.

None of that mattered

back then

not even the cold

linoleum floors.

Did everyone

have linoleum?

It was okay then

to get up early

or

at least

we were not scolded for long.

Christmas came

    and went back then

  as it does for most kids.

Searching through

    my mind,

  I can't remember much more

      about those mornings---

  Rice Krispies and milk

and my feet

  on the cold linoleum floors.

1995

CHRISTMAS LIGHTS

The leaves

  aren't quite covered

    yet.

The colors still

  shine

    through

  the snow,

    almost

  melting the flakes

    as they fall.

The cold and wind

    have stayed away,

      the snow

tries to build

       a blanket

  to hide

what the trees gave away.

We always wish

       for the snow

  this day, but

I'm glad the leaves

       won.

The colors feel

  so much warmer

     now,

    more like lights

glimmering among the trees.

1998

TOYS **R** US

Do you really

        think

      Christmas is about

        toys?

I think I thought

   that. At least

at one time I did.

I learned

   the true meaning

      of Christmas,

   way back then.

I mean I know,

   but the toys

were Christmas.

I haven't received
   any toys in many years,
I don't even believe
      I still have any.

Does someone
   give them back
      or, do they just
         disappear?

I wouldn't want that---
      you know,
   the disappearing part.

I guess I should
      just believe that
   Christmas is magic.

The magic that comes

    and goes within us.

  It doesn't need

      to be real,

   imaginary

      or even seen.

Just as long as you—

   believe.

Never let it disappear

  no matter where

    the toys **R**.

CHANGING COLORS

Walking,

the leaves crunch

under the weight

of my feet.

The sounds,

we've grown to know.

On this clear day,

as the bright sun

shines through

the trees,

the reds, yellows, oranges, greens

color my thoughts.

For sure,

winter

lies ahead.

The leaves will

give way

and the snow

will fall.

The shy has changed

and the blowing wind,

has moved the colors

behind doors.

Inside, the trees

are green

covered by the color

of lights and dreams.

They replace the fallen

leaves

reds, yellows, oranges…

127

I'll miss the fall,

    as I always do.

        But,

            it gives us

        the winter.

Passing into spring,

        with a short

    stop at Christmas.

A brief moment in time,

    between the

        changing colors.

1999

ICE CRYSTALS

The rains have

          slowed,

     to that faint drizzle

         my face

   can't escape.

The cold holds the drops

     that freeze, building

  as they land

       on the ground.

The snow becomes entombed

     with no escape. Covered,

       guarded, protected

  by the frozen mist.

Ice Crystals crack

          under my very

               steps.

As the sun's

        light struggles,

     stealing the sky…

The ice won.

Covered,

     the glitter takes over

         once the rain

             passes.

For the moment,

     we succumb in awe,

        to the **"Ice Crystals."**

2002

THE WREATH ON THE DOOR

The smell in

the air,

is just about gone.

Needles

have already started

falling.

Opening the door,

the wind blowing

dropping them to my feet.

Weeks ago,

the smell came

back

I looked for that hook

realizing,

there never was.

A way is found,

captured

but,

a promise never kept.

Each year,

meaning to get something,

planning

and

each year waiting

for the next.

The smell again

will return.

Needles fall

as the wind blows

in the open door.

Each year,

    looking to the next…

As the door is closed,

    the smell is gone.

THE CHRISTMAS CARD

Little snow

is forecasted,

as I walk

to the box.

Most days,

this time

of year,

it's easy to be

reminded

of friends,

family

and so much more.

You sort through

the pile

you hold

looking, reading

and

figuring out

those return addresses.

Who sent them,

who remembered,

who didn't,

and those that

couldn't, but

you remember.

The cards are

the way we

remember,

and will remember

and remember…

2004

THE CREEK

Earlier today

the sounds

could be heard.

Water running

as it flows

over the rocks.

The snow from the trees

dropping in clumps,

melting,

adding to the sounds.

The creek is usually

frozen by 'Christmas'

most years.

Sounds heard

at winter's end.

A tree had fallen

from winters back.

The weight

of a storm,

long past.

They say

the cold weather

isn't

far away.

Perhaps!

Tomorrow

the creek

will slow again,

freeze…

and 'Christmas' comes,

the day after that.

Made in the USA
Columbia, SC
28 April 2025

72b29d8a-eff5-4c7f-99fb-49c4ec235bcfR01